GRUMBUG!

Trolliver's CAFÉ

Adam Stower

This is Oliver…

Oliver has a little sister, Dolly.

This is NOT Dolly.

This is Troll,

Oliver's best friend.

This is Dolly!

Oliver and Troll
run their own café in the woods.
It is an unusual café. It is not a café for
people at all. It is a café for…

café

OPEN

trollivers
CAFÉ

Now, everybody knows
that normally trolls eat children.

But not THESE trolls.

These trolls prefer Oliver's cakes because they
taste much nicer and are a lot easier to catch.
(Trolls are a lazy bunch!)

One day Oliver and Troll baked a fresh batch
of their special TRIPLE TREACLE TROLL TREATS!

The café was jam-packed.

Oliver and Troll were SO busy,

that it was quite some time before they noticed…

...Dolly was MISSING!

DOLLY?

Oliver and Troll
searched the café
from top to bottom.

But Dolly had vanished.

THERE'S NOWHERE HERE
FOR HER TO HIDE,
LET'S GO AND TAKE
A LOOK OUTSIDE.

The trolls all gasped and turned to stare,
then a wise old troll called out:

BEWARE!
STEER CLEAR OF MUNCH MOUNTAIN—
YOU KNOW WHO LIVES THERE!

Scoffing at their silliness,
Oliver untied his apron
and put on his boots.

He'd met all sorts of trolls
but NONE as bad as that.

And this GRUMBUG would be no different.

WE'LL TAKE A CAKE
SO IF WE MEET,
HE'LL HAVE SOMETHING
NICER THAN US TO EAT.

NOW LET'S GO!
WHO'S COMING?

Suddenly everyone was terribly busy.

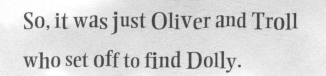

So, it was just Oliver and Troll
who set off to find Dolly.

They were soon on
the right track.

Troll followed gingerly

as Oliver skipped on ahead.

With that, Oliver marched on.

Still Troll followed timidly behind...

...because Dolly's trail was leading them straight to MUNCH MOUNTAIN!

Up and up they climbed.

And at the top,
guess what they found...?

…a smiling Dolly, safe and sound!

OLIBA!

But then they heard they weren't alone.

From a dark cave there came a moan,

and the grumble of a rumbling stomach…

Was this the BIGGEST, MEANEST,

GRUMPIEST and GREENEST

troll of ALL?

Oliver grabbed the cake and said:

DON'T EAT US, EAT **THIS** INSTEAD!

A little crumbly voice replied:

OH, HOW SPLENDID! WHAT A TREAT! CAKES IS WHAT I LOVES TO EAT!

Oliver, Troll and Dolly ran as fast as they could,

all the way down Munch Mountain.

And they didn't stop running until they were home again.